THE CRANKYPANTS TEA PARTY

written by Barbara Bottner

illustrated by Ale Barba

A Caitlyn Dlouhy Book

A atheneum Atheneum Books for Young Readers
New York • London • Toronto • Sydney • New Delhi

To all the Crankies. I understand. I really do.

—B. B.

To Sofi, who wanted to join the party.

I was so happy to see you around.

—A. B.

atheneum ATHENEUM BOOKS FOR YOUNG READERS • An imprint of Simon & Schuster Children's Publishing Division • 1230 Avenue of the Americas, New York, New York 10020 • Text copyright © 2020 by Barbara Bottner • Illustrations copyright © 2020 by Ale Barba • All rights reserved, including the right of reproduction in whole or in part in any form. • ATHENEUM BOOKS FOR YOUNG READERS is a registered trademark of Simon & Schuster, Inc. Atheneum logo is a trademark of Simon & Schuster, Inc. • For information about special discounts for bulk purchases, please contact Simon & Schuster Special Sales at 1-866-506-1949 or business@simonandschuster.com. • The Simon & Schuster Speakers Bureau can bring authors to your live event. For more information or to book an event, contact the Simon & Schuster Speakers Bureau at 1-866-248-3049 or visit our website at www.simonspeakers.com. • Book design by Semadar Megged • The text for this book was set in Carrotflower • The illustrations for this book were rendered in acrylics • Manufactured in China · 0320 SCP • First Edition • 10 9 8 7 6 5 4 3 2 1 • Library of Congress Cataloging-in-Publication Data • Names: Bottner, Barbara, author. | Barba, Ale, illustrator. • Title: The Crankypants tea party / Barbara Bottner ; illustrated by Ale Barba. • Description: First edition. | New York : Atheneum Books for Young Readers, 2020. | Audience: Ages 4–8. | Audience: Grades K–1. | Summary: Clarissa invites all of her stuffed animals to a tea party, but they refuse to attend because they think she has mistreated them. • Identifiers: LCCN 2019035655 | ISBN 9781481459006 (hardcover) | ISBN 9781481459013 (eBook) • Subjects: CYAC: Toys—Fiction. | Parties—Fiction. | Afternoon teas—Fiction. • Classification: LCC PZ7.B6586 Cr 2020 | DDC [E]—dc23 | LC record available at https://lccn.loc.gov/2019035655

Clarissa:
What a beautiful day!
It's perfect for a
tea party!

All stuffed animals:

NO THANK YOU!

Clarissa: But I insist! I'm setting the table, and you're all invited.

Elephant: I'm not interested! Last time, the ice cream melted on my head.

Pup: But she washed you off.

Monkey: Elephant likes to be clean.

Elephant: But the washcloth was too rough. And she got soap in my eye.

Pup: Elephant's a big baby.

Pig: At least Clarissa plays with *him*.

Clarissa: Let's get started.
Who's going to bring the chairs?

Rabbit: Not me. Nuh-uh. You left me outside. I'm still damp.

Pig: I'm losing my stuffing. BECAUSE OF YOU!

Clarissa: But I pinned you back together!
Now, who wants to fold the napkins?

Monkey: You tied knots in my shoelaces.
I fell down twice!

Bear: I don't want tea. You forgot about
me all week!

Pig: You made me go to bed.

Monkey: When he wasn't even tired!

Rabbit: And you made me wear a hat. . . . Look at my ear!

Clarissa: I thought the hat looked adorable!
And I'LL sew your ear after the tea party.

Bear: Oh! Queen Clarissa says AFTER THE TEA PARTY. Of course!

Clarissa: Poor darlings. You're all a big bunch of CRANKYPANTS!

Monkey: She doesn't understand a thing!
I'm getting WET!

All: Let's ignore her. Maybe THEN
she'll learn to appreciate us.

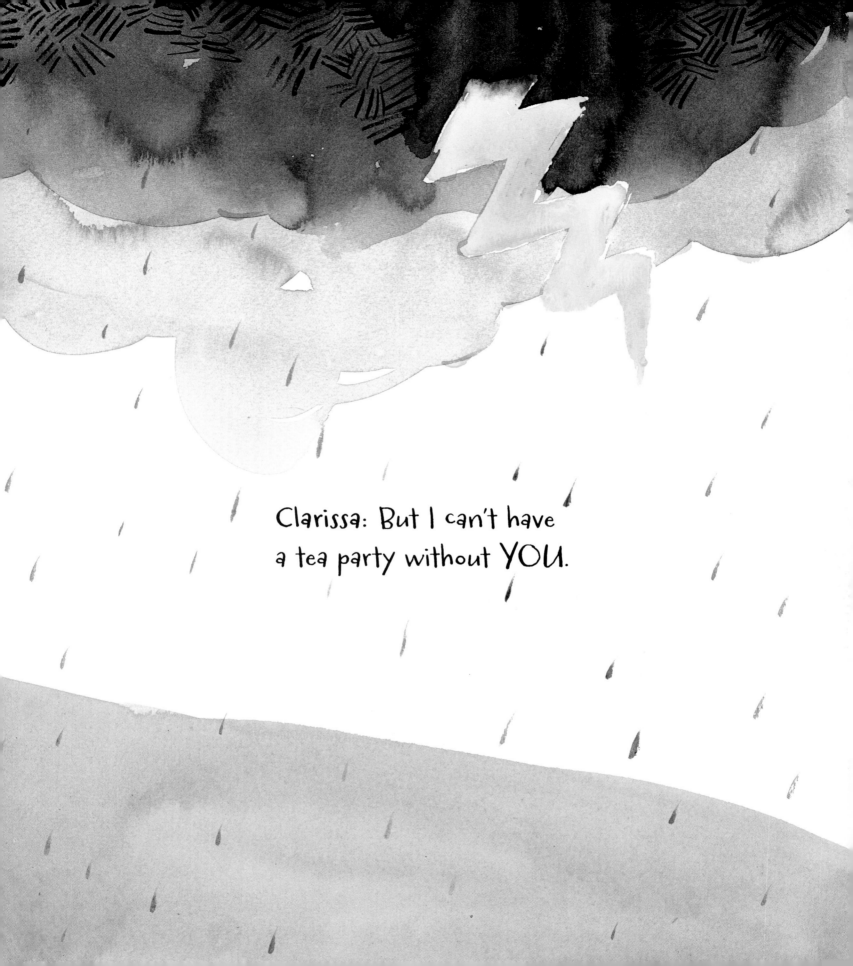

Clarissa: But I can't have
a tea party without YOU.

All: POOR, POOR CLARISSA!

Monkey: I say, who needs Queen Clarissa anyway?

Rabbit: Or her dumb tea parties?

Pig: I don't.

Bear: Me neither. I don't even miss her!

All (except Pup): Nope!

Pup: Hey, it's really dark! I wish Clarissa were here!

Pig & Elephant: Since when does Pup have a say?

Rabbit: He's her favorite.

Bear: I thought *I* was her favorite.

Clarissa: Let me explain.

Elephant loves ice cream, so
I shared mine and it melted.
So I had to clean him up.

I left Rabbit outside because he said he enjoyed the breeze.

I only tied knots in Monkey's shoes to keep him from losing them.

I didn't forget Bear. I was saving him for his birthday next week.

And Pig got torn because he plays too rough! Then he was falling asleep on the rug, so I put him to bed.

All (except pup): She always has excuses!

PUP: Wait, wait, wait! Did you forget? She serves milk at four. And soup du jour.

Monkey: Quite yummy!

Clarissa: And I sing you songs and lullabies.

Rabbit: Clarissa *does* give the best cuddles.

Elephant: But then she wants to kiss us.

Rabbit: KISSES!

Pig & Bear: Kisses!

Clarissa: I thought you loved kisses.

Monkey: Not every day!

Pup: I do love a good-night kiss.

Bear: Me too!

Elephant, Rabbit, Pig: Me too, me too!

Clarissa: Well, then, it's settled!
          We're having a tea party!!

Pup: I'm helping!

Elephant: No, I am!

Bear: I'LL set the table!

Monkey: That's my job! I always set the table.

Bear: Then, I can fold the napkins!

Rabbit: But I am the neatest. I'll fold the napkins.
Bear can arrange the chairs!

Bear: Arranging the chairs is too boring.

Elephant: I like arranging the chairs.

Pup: Then, what will I do?

Monkey: You can open the tablecloth.

Bear: Excuse me. I get to open the tablecloth.

Pup: Then, I'll cut the cake?

All: Pup, you always get to cut the cake!

Clarissa: No more complaining,
Crankypants! Tea-party manners, please!
Pig: I already have good manners.
Rabbit: I have the best manners.
Monkey: No, you don't.
Pass the sugar.
Pup: You mean "please" pass the sugar.
Monkey: Yes, please.
Bear: I love a good tea party.
Pup: Thank you, Clarissa.

ALL: Thank you, Clarissa.